The

Storybook
Collection

The Tiny Seed

Pancakes, Pancakes!

The Mountain That Loved a Bird

Walter the Baker

A House for Hermit Crab

The Greedy Python

Rooster Off to See the World

Simon & Schuster Books for Young Readers
Simon & Schuster
New York

Eric Carle

The Tiny Seed

It is Autumn.
A strong wind is blowing. It blows flower seeds high in the air and carries them far across the land. One of the seeds is tiny, smaller than any of the others. Will it be able to keep up with the others? And where are they all going?

One of the seeds flies higher than the others. Up, up it goes! It flies too high and the sun's hot rays burn it up. But the tiny seed sails on with the others.

Another seed lands on a tall and icy mountain.
The ice never melts, and the seed cannot grow.
The rest of the seeds fly on. But the tiny seed
does not go as fast as the others.

Now they fly over the ocean. One seed falls into the water and drowns. The others sail on with the wind. But the tiny seed does not go as high as the others.

One seed drifts down onto the desert. It is hot and dry, and the seed cannot grow. Now the tiny seed is flying very low, but the wind pushes it on with the others.

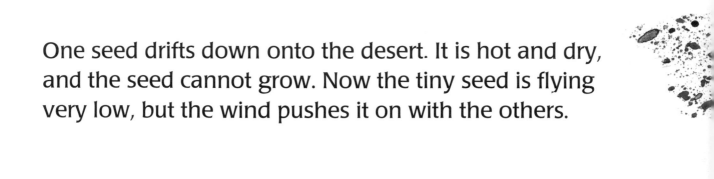
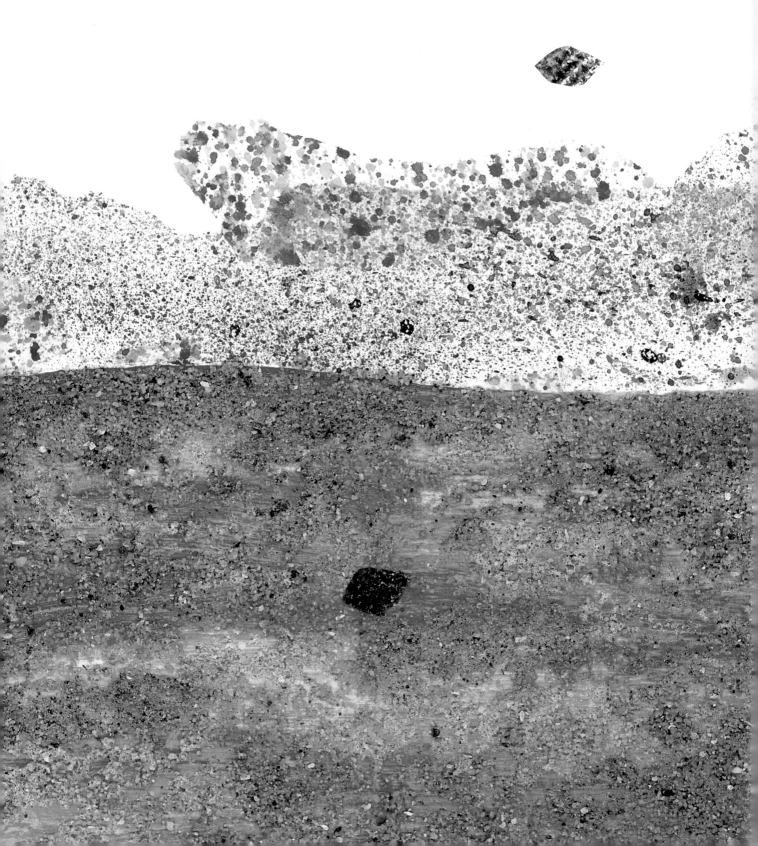

Finally the wind stops and the seeds fall gently down on the ground. A bird comes by and eats one seed. The tiny seed is not eaten. It is so small that the bird does not see it.

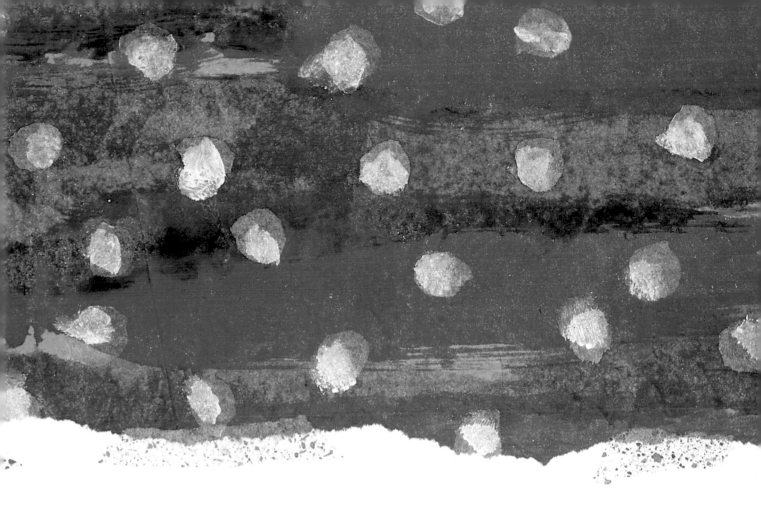

Now it is Winter.
After their long trip the seeds settle down. They look just as if they are going to sleep in the earth. Snow falls and covers them like a soft white blanket. A hungry mouse that also lives in the ground eats a seed for his lunch. But the tiny seed lies very still and the mouse does not see it.

Now it is Spring.
After a few months the snow has melted. It is really spring!
Birds fly by. The sun shines. Rain falls. The seeds grow so
round and full they start to burst open a little.
Now they are not seeds any more. They are plants. First
they send roots down into the earth. Then their little stems
and leaves begin to grow up toward the sun and air.
There is another plant that grows much faster than the
new little plants. It is a big fat weed. And it takes all the
sunlight and the rain away from one of the small new
plants. And that little plant dies.

The tiny seed hasn't begun to grow yet. It will be too late!
Hurry! But finally it too starts to grow into a plant.

The warm weather also brings the children out to play.
They too have been waiting for the sun and spring time.
One child doesn't see the plants as he runs along and —
Oh! He breaks one! Now it cannot grow any more.

The tiny plant that grew from the tiny seed is growing fast, but its neighbor grows even faster. Before the tiny plant has three leaves the other plant has seven! And look! A bud! And now even a flower!

But what is happening? First there are footsteps. Then a shadow looms over them. Then a hand reaches down and breaks off the flower.

A boy has picked the flower to give to a friend.

It is Summer.
Now the tiny plant from the tiny seed is all alone.
It grows on and on. It doesn't stop. The sun shines
on it and the rain waters it. It has many leaves.
It grows taller and taller. It is taller than the people.
It is taller than the trees. It is taller than the houses.
And now a flower grows on it. People come from
far and near to look at this flower. It is the tallest
flower they have ever seen. It is a giant flower.

All summer long the birds and bees and butterflies come visiting. They have never seen such a big and beautiful flower.

Now it is Autumn again.
The days grow shorter. The nights grow cooler. And
the wind carries yellow and red leaves past the flower.
Some petals drop from the giant flower and they sail
along with the bright leaves over the land and down
to the ground.

The wind blows harder. The flower has lost almost all of its petals. It sways and bends away from the wind. But the wind grows stronger and shakes the flower. Once more the wind shakes the flower, and this time the flower's seed pod opens. Out come many tiny seeds that quickly sail far away on the wind.

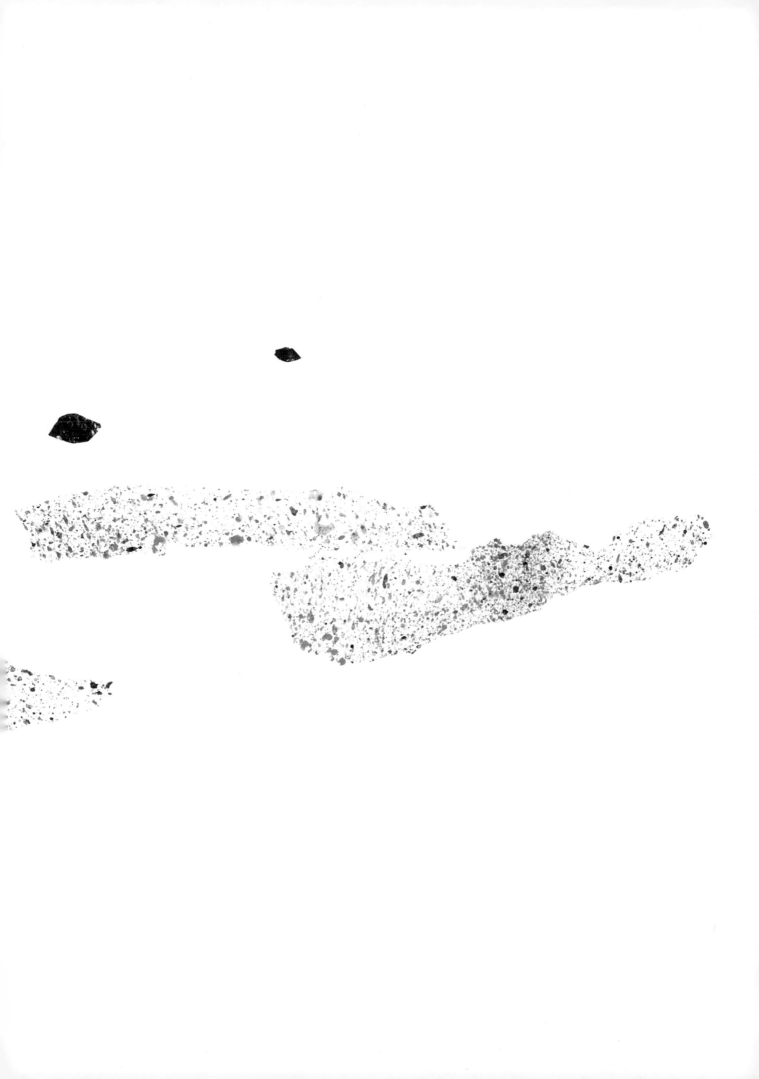

Pancakes,
Pancakes!

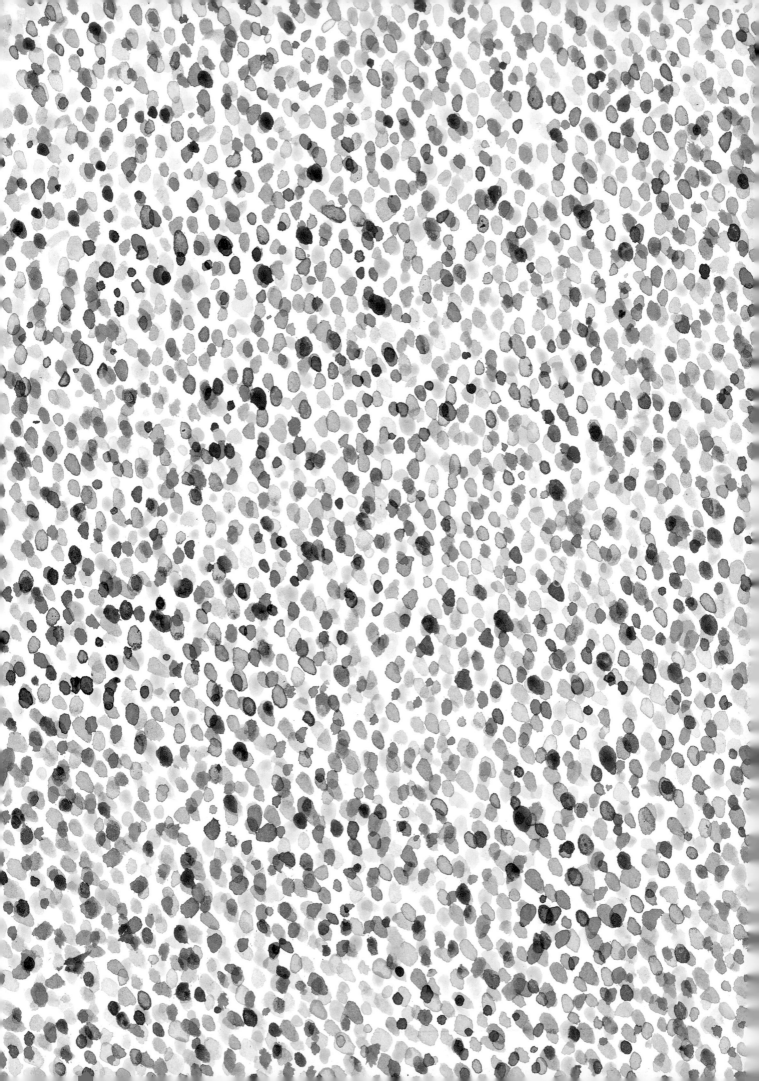

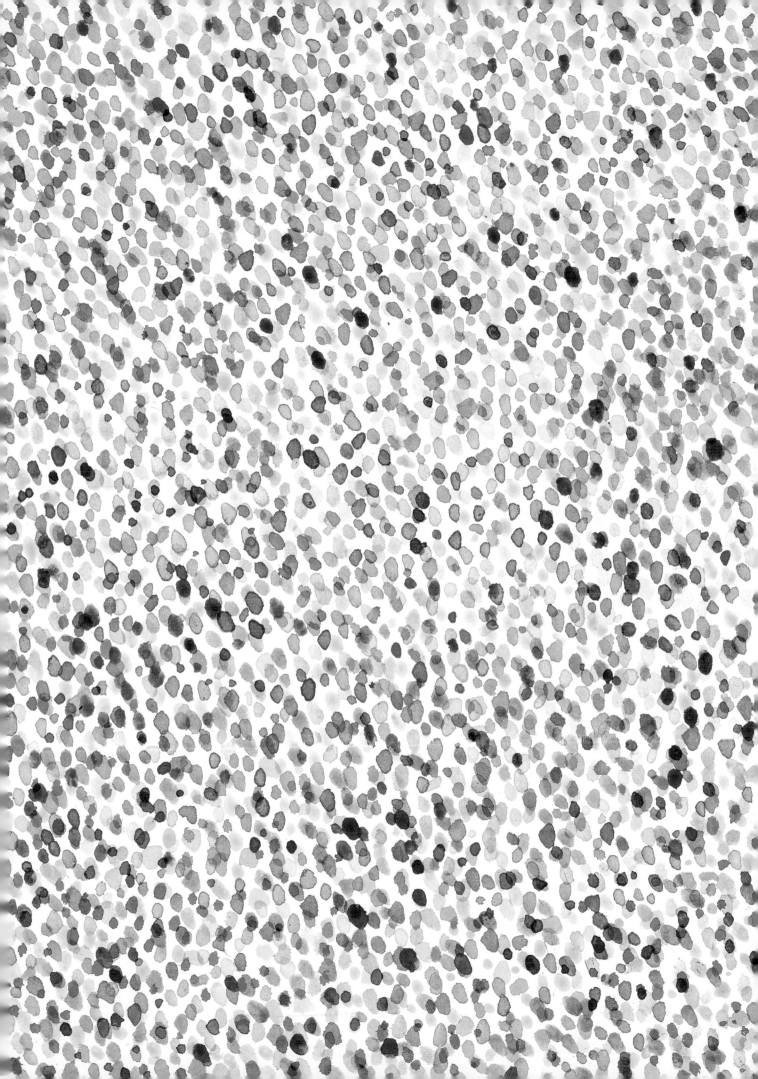

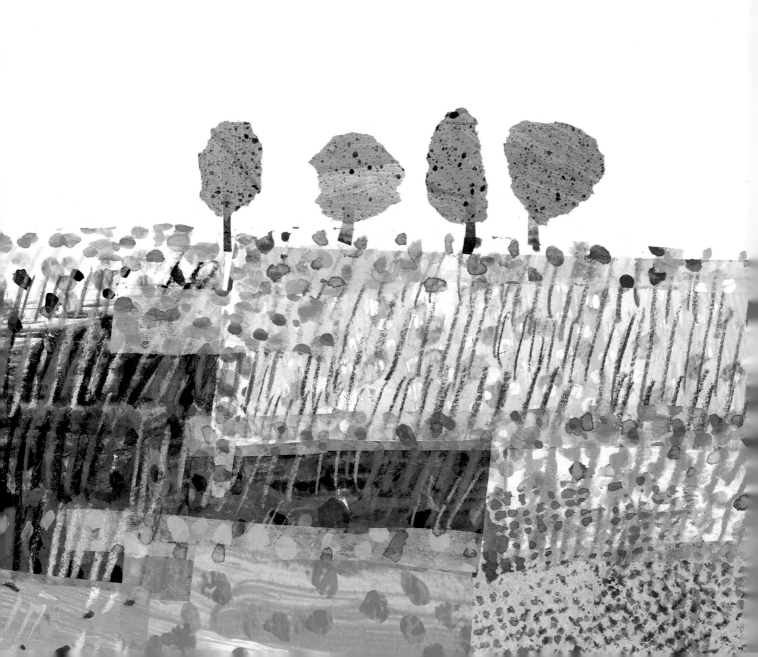

Pancakes, Pancakes!

Kee-ke-ri-kee

crowed the rooster.
Jack woke up, looked out
the window and thought,
"I'd like to have a
big pancake for breakfast."

Jack's mother was already up and busy.
"Mother," said Jack, "I'd like to have a big pancake for breakfast."
"I am busy and you will have to help me," she said.
"How can I help?" asked Jack.
"We'll need some flour," she replied.

"Take a sickle and cut as much wheat as the donkey can carry.
Then take it to the mill. The miller will grind it into flour."

When Jack had cut enough wheat,
he put it on the donkey's back and took it to the miller.

"Can you grind this wheat for me?" he asked.
"I need it for a big pancake."
"First we must separate the grain from the chaff," said the miller.

He gave Jack a flail and spread the wheat onto the ground.
The miller took another flail and began to beat the wheat with it.
Jack helped with the threshing,
and soon there was a big pile of straw and chaff—
and a small pile of grain.

The miller poured the grain on a large flat stone.
On top of it was a round millstone
connected to the water wheel on the outside.
The water wheel turned round and round,
turning the millstone round and round, too,
to grind the grain into flour.
At last the miller handed Jack a bag of flour.

"Here's the flour," shouted Jack. "Let's make a pancake."
But his mother said, "Now we need an egg."
Jack went to the black hen and fed her some grain that had slipped
into his pocket while he had been threshing.
"Cluck, cluck," said the black hen and went inside the hen house.
Then she said, "Cluck, cluck," once more and laid an egg.

"Here's an egg," shouted Jack. "Let's make a pancake."
But his mother said, "Now we need some milk."
Jack went to the spotted cow and began to milk her.
"Moo, moo," said the spotted cow as the milk squirted into the pail.

"Here's the milk," shouted Jack. "Let's make a pancake."
But his mother said, "We need some butter."
Jack got the butter churn and held it between his knees.
His mother scooped the cream from the top of the milk
and put it into the butter churn.
Jack pushed the churn handle up and down, up and down.
Finally, the cream turned into butter.

"Here's the butter," shouted Jack. "let's make a pancake."
But his mother said, "We need to build a fire."
Jack went to the woodshed and brought some firewood.

"Here's the firewood," shouted Jack. "Let's make a pancake."
But his mother said,
"Wouldn't you like to have something sweet on your pancake?"
So Jack went down to the cool cellar
and pulled a jar of strawberry jam from one of the shelves.

"Here's the strawberry jam," shouted Jack.
"Let's make a pancake."
In the kitchen, Jack's mother had filled the table with
the flour,
the egg,
the milk,
the butter.

There was also
a mixing bowl,
a cup,
a wooden spoon,
a ladle,
a frying pan,
a plate,
a knife, fork, and spoon.
And a jar of strawberry jam.

And his mother said, "Put a cupful of flour into the bowl...

"Break an egg into the flour and stir...

"Pour a cupful of milk over the flour and eggs and stir again until the batter is smooth and without lumps."

Jack's mother heated the frying pan over the fire,
and added a piece of butter. The butter melted fast.

Then she said to Jack,
"Now pour a ladleful of batter into the hot pan."

After a minute or two she looked at the underside of the pancake.
It was golden brown.
"Now watch," she said, "I'll turn the pancake over. Ready?"

"Ready!" shouted Jack.
"Flip," said his mother.
Up and over went the pancake high into the air
and landed right in the pan. In another minute or two
the pancake was crisp on the underside as well.

Then she slipped the pancake from the frying pan onto the plate
and spread some strawberry jam on it.
"And now, Jack," his mother started to say,
but Jack said…

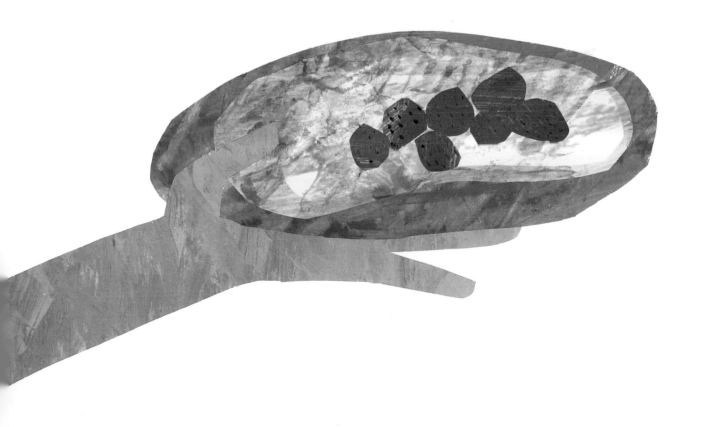

"Oh, Mama, I know what to do now!"

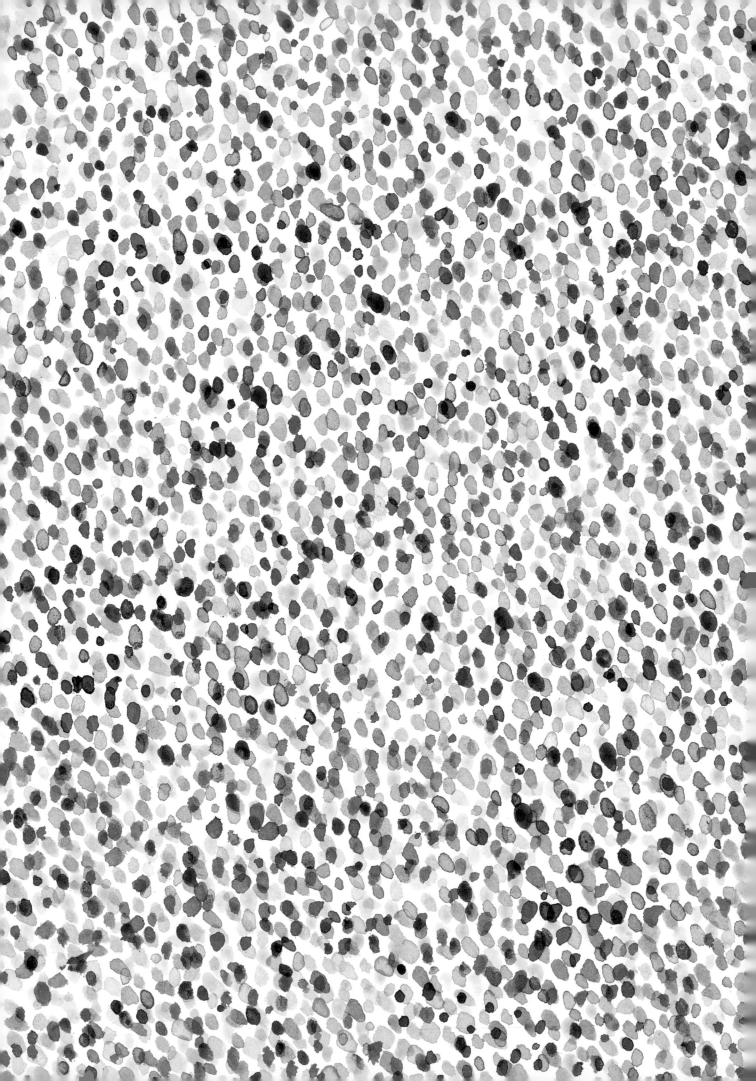

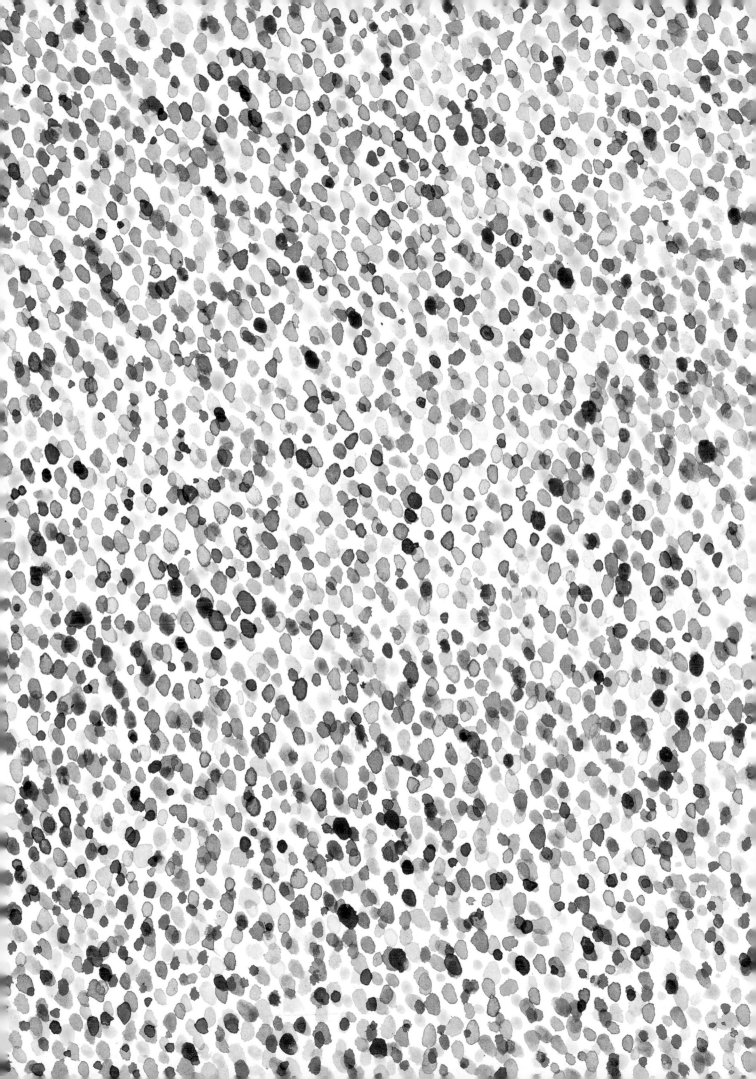

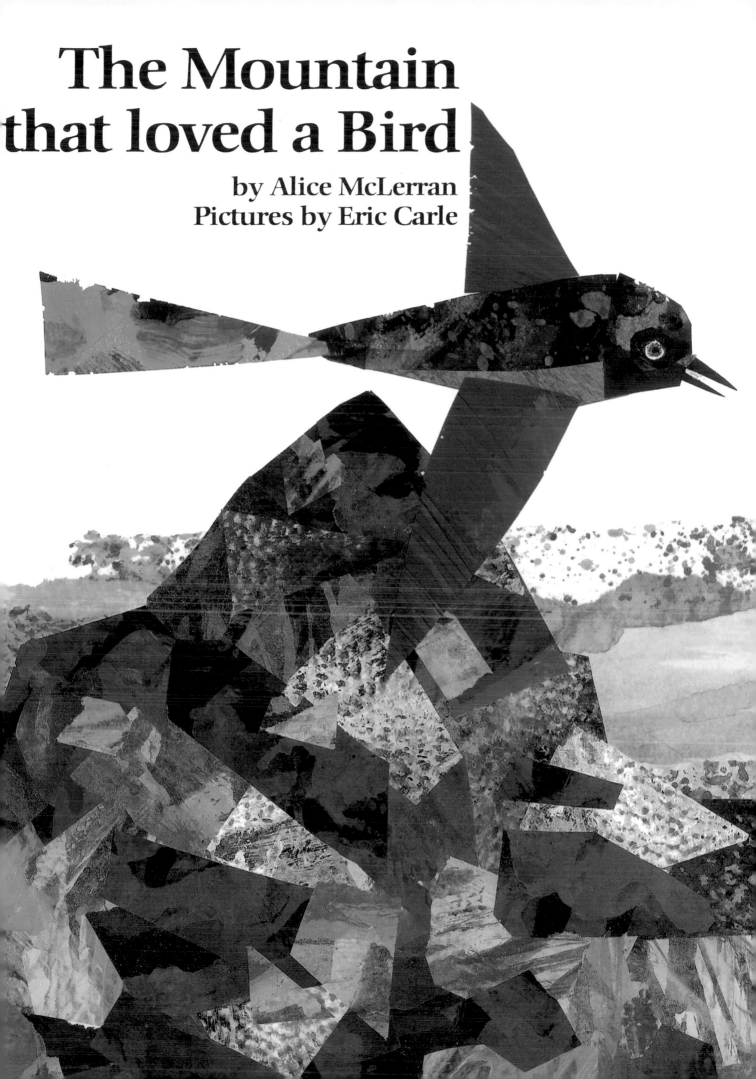

The Mountain
that loved a Bird

by Alice McLerran
Pictures by Eric Carle

The Mountain That Loved a Bird

by Alice McLerran
Pictures by Eric Carle

There was once a mountain made of bare stone.
It stood alone in the middle of a desert plain. No plant grew on its hard slopes, nor could any animal, bird or insect live there.

The sun warmed the mountain and the wind chilled it, but the only touch the mountain knew was the touch of rain or snow.
There was nothing more to feel.

All day and all night the mountain looked only at the sky, watching for
the movement of the billowing clouds. It knew the path of the sun that
crossed the sky by day, and the course of the moon that crossed the sky
by night. On clear nights, it watched the slow wheeling of the far-off stars.
There was nothing more to see.

But then one day a small bird appeared. She flew in a circle above the mountain, then landed on a ledge to rest and preen her feathers. The mountain felt the dry grasp of her tiny claws on the ledge; it felt the softness of her feathered body as she sheltered herself against its side. The mountain was amazed, for nothing like this had ever come to it from the sky before.

"Who are you?" the mountain asked. "What is your name?"

"I am a bird," replied the other. "My name is Joy, and I come from distant lands, where everything is green. Every spring I fly high into the air, looking for the best place to build my nest and raise my children. As soon as I have rested I must continue my search."

"I have never seen anything like you before," said the mountain. "Must you go on? Couldn't you just stay here?"

Joy shook her head. "Birds are living things," she explained. "We must have food and water. Nothing grows here for me to eat; there are no streams from which I could drink."

"If you cannot stay here, will you come back again some day?" asked the mountain.

Joy thought for a while. "I fly long distances," she said, "and I have rested on many mountains. No other mountain has ever cared whether I came or went, and I should like to return to you. But I could only do so in the spring before I build my nest, and because you are so far from food and water I could only stay a few hours."

"I have never seen anything like you before," repeated the mountain. "Even if it were only for a few hours, it would make me happy to see you again."

"There is one more thing you should know," said Joy. "Mountains last forever, but birds do not. Even if I were to visit you every spring of my life, there might be only a few visits. Birds do not live very many years."

"It will be very sad when your visits stop," said the mountain, "but it would be even sadder if you fly away now and never return."

Joy sat very still, nestled against the side of the mountain. Then she began to sing a gentle, bell-like song, the first music the mountain had ever heard. When she had finished her song, she said, "Because no mountain has ever before cared whether I came or went, I will make you a promise. Every spring of my life, I will return to greet you, and fly above you, and sing to you. And since my life will not last forever, I will give to one of my daughters my own name, Joy, and tell her how to find you. And she will name a daughter Joy also, and tell her how to find you. Each Joy will have a daughter Joy, so that no matter how many years pass, you will always have a friend to greet you and fly above you and sing to you."

The mountain was both happy and sad. "I still wish you could stay," it said, "but I am glad you will return."

"Now I must go," said Joy, "for it is a long way to the lands that have food and water for me. Goodbye until next year."
She soared off, her wings like feathered fans against the sun.
The mountain watched her until she disappeared into the distance.

Year after year, when every spring came, a small bird flew to the mountain, singing, "I am Joy, and I have come to greet you." And for a few hours, the bird would fly above the mountain, or nestle against its side, singing. At the end of each visit, the mountain always asked, "Isn't there some way you could stay?" And Joy always answered, "No, but I will return next year."

Each year the mountain looked forward more and more to Joy's visit; each year it grew harder and harder to watch her go. Ninety-nine springs came and went in this way. On the hundredth spring, when it was time for Joy to leave, the mountain asked once more, "Isn't there some way you could stay?" Joy answered, as she always did, "No, but I will return next year." The mountain watched as she disappeared into the sky, and suddenly its heart broke. The hard stone cracked, and from the deepest part of the mountain tears gushed forth and rolled down the mountainside in a stream.

The next spring a small bird appeared, singing, "I am Joy, and I have come to greet you." This time the mountain did not reply. It only wept, thinking of how soon she would have to leave, and of all the long months before she would come again. Joy rested on her ledge, and looked at the stream of tears. Then she flew above the mountain, and sang as she always had. When it was time for her to go, the mountain still wept. "I will return next year," said Joy softly, and she flew away.

When the next spring came, Joy
returned, carrying in her beak a small
seed. The mountain still wept a stream
of tears. Joy carefully tucked the seed
into a crack in the hard stone, close
to the stream so that it would stay
moist. Then she flew above the
mountain, and sang to it. Seeing that
the mountain was still unable to speak,
she flew away once more.

During the weeks that followed, the seed in the crack of the rock began to send down tiny roots. The roots reached into the hard stone, little by little spreading into yet smaller cracks, breaking through the hardness. As the roots found water in the cracks, and drew food from the softening stone, a shoot rose from the seed into the sunlight and unfolded tiny green leaves. The mountain, however, was still deep in sorrow, blind with tears. It did not notice a plant so small.

The next spring Joy brought another seed, and the spring after that another. She placed each one in a protected place near the stream of tears, and sang to the mountain. The mountain still only wept.

Years passed in this way, the roots of new plants softening the stone near the stream of tears. As softened stone turned to soil, moss began to grow in sheltered corners. Grasses and little flowering plants sprouted in hollows near the stream. Tiny insects, carried to the mountain by the winds, scurried among the leaves.

Meanwhile, the roots of the very first seed went deeper and deeper into the heart of the mountain. Above the ground, what had started as a tiny shoot was growing into the trunk of a young tree, its branches holding green leaves out to the sun. At last, the mountain felt the roots reaching down like gentle fingers, filling and healing the cracks in its heart. Sorrow faded away, and the mountain began to notice the changes that had been taking place. So varied and wondrous were all these things, the mountain's tears changed to tears of happiness.

Each year Joy returned, bringing another seed. Each year, more streams ran laughing down the mountain's sides, and the ground watered by the new streams grew green with trees and other plants.

Now that the mountain no longer wept with sorrow, it began to ask once more, "Isn't there some way you could stay?" But Joy still answered, "No, but I will return next year."

More years passed, and the streams carried life far out into the plain surrounding the mountain, until finally, as far as the mountain could see, everything was green. From lands beyond the horizon, small animals began to come to the mountain. Watching these living things find food and shelter on its slopes, the mountain suddenly felt a surge of hope. Opening its deepest heart to the roots of the trees, it offered them all its strength. The trees stretched their branches yet higher toward the sky, and hope ran like a song from the heart of the mountain into every tree leaf.

And sure enough, when the next spring came,
Joy flew to the mountain carrying not a seed,
but a slender twig. Straight to the tallest tree
on the mountain she flew, to the tree that had
grown from the very first seed. She placed the
twig on the branch in which she would build her nest.
"I am Joy," she sang, "and I have come to stay."

Walter the Baker

Walter the Baker

For my mother and father

Walter the Baker

Long ago, in a town encircled by a wall,
lived Walter the Baker, his wife Anna, and their son Walter Jr.

Walter the Baker was known even outside the walls of the town.
He was the best baker in the whole Duchy.
Early every morning, while everybody else was still asleep,
Walter began baking his breads, rolls, cookies, tarts, and pies.

Anna sold the baked goods in the store.
No one could resist the warm, sweet smells drifting from Walter's bakery.
People came from near and far.

The Duke and Duchess who ruled over the Duchy
loved Walter's sweet rolls.
Every morning Walter Jr. carried a basketful of warm sweet rolls
to the castle where they lived.

"Mm," said the Duchess, spreading quince jelly on her roll.
"Ahh," said the Duke, putting honey on his.
  And so each day was the same as the day before—
                              until one early morning…

…when Walter's cat was chasing a mouse and tipped over the can of milk.
"What will I do?" cried Walter.
"I cannot make sweet rolls without fresh milk."
In desperation, Walter grabbed a pitcher of water.
"I hope nobody will notice the difference," he said
as he poured the water into the flour to make the dough.

Now, you and I may not be able to tell the difference between a roll made with water and one made with milk.

But the Duke and especially the Duchess could tell the difference.

"Ugh," cried the Duchess after she took a bite.

"What is this!" roared the Duke.

"Where is Walter the Baker? Bring him here at once!"

So Walter was brought before the Duke.

"What do you call this?" roared the Duke.

"This is not a roll, this is a stone!" And with that he threw it at Walter's feet.

"I used water instead of milk," Walter admitted, hanging his head in shame.

"Pack your things and leave this town and my Duchy forever,"
shouted the Duke. "I never want to see you again!"

"My Duke," pleaded Walter, "this is my home. Where will I go?
Please give me one more chance, please."

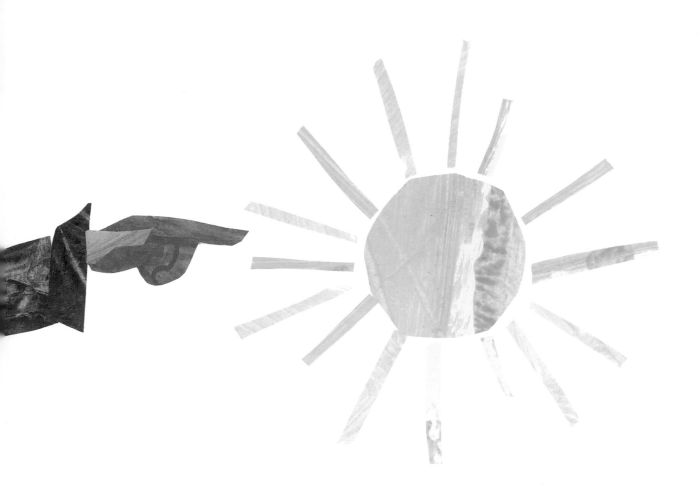

"I must banish you," said the Duke.
But then he remembered Walter's good rolls and how much he
and the Duchess would miss them.
"Well, Walter…" the Duke started to say.
Then he thought and thought some more.
"You may stay if you can invent a roll through which the rising sun
can shine three times."
And to make it more difficult, he added, "It must be made from
one piece of dough, and most of all, it must taste good.
Now go home and bring me such a roll tomorrow morning."
Poor Walter! Worried and sad, he trudged back to his bakery.

Walter worked all day and into the night.
He made long rolls, short rolls, round rolls, twisted rolls.
He made thin rolls and he made fat rolls.
And he worked some more.

Walter beat, pulled, pushed, and pounded the dough.

But it was all in vain.

He could not come up with a roll that would please the Duke.
By early morning Walter had only one long piece of dough left.
"It's hopeless," he cried.
In a sudden fit of anger, he grabbed the last piece of dough
and flung it against the ceiling.
"Stick there!" he yelled at the dough.
But it didn't. It fell, twisting itself as it dropped down
and plopped into a pail of water.

Anna and Walter Jr. were awakened by Walter's yell and
rushed into the bakery just as Walter was about to dump out
the water and the twisted piece of dough.
"Father, stop!" shouted Walter Jr. "Look!"

And Anna quickly popped the dough into the hot oven.
Soon it was brown and crisp.
She took out the roll and handed it to Walter.
It hadn't risen very high, but it had three holes.

Walter held up the twisted roll and smiled.
He saw that the morning sun was shining through it three times.

Walter put the roll into a basket and rushed to the castle
to deliver his invention to the Duke and Duchess.
And they too saw the morning sun shine through it three times.
Then the Duke and Duchess each took a small bite.
·Walter was afraid to look, because he had no idea how it would taste.
"Well done!" said the Duke.
"Perfect!" exclaimed the Duchess.
Both were glad that Walter would not have to be sent away.

And Walter too was happy that he could stay.
"Now, pray tell us, Walter. What do you call this?" asked the Duke.
"Uh, yes, pray us tell…" Walter stammered, as he tried to come up with a name.
"What was that? Pra… pre… pretzel?" said the Duke. "Pretzel it shall be.
From now on," he declared, "it shall be sweet rolls in the morning…"
"… and pretzels in the afternoon," said the Duchess.

Walter returned to his bakery and spent all day and night making pretzels. The next morning there were baskets of pretzels outside the store for the whole town to taste.

And a special basket of pretzels for the Duke and Duchess.

And a cheer went up for Walter the Pretzel Maker.

The word pretzel comes from the Latin word bracchium, meaning "arm."
The pretzel was originally a simple bread eaten during Lent. Its shape is based
on an ancient position for prayer in which the arms were folded across
the chest and the hands were placed on opposite shoulders.

A House for Hermit Crab

Eric Carle

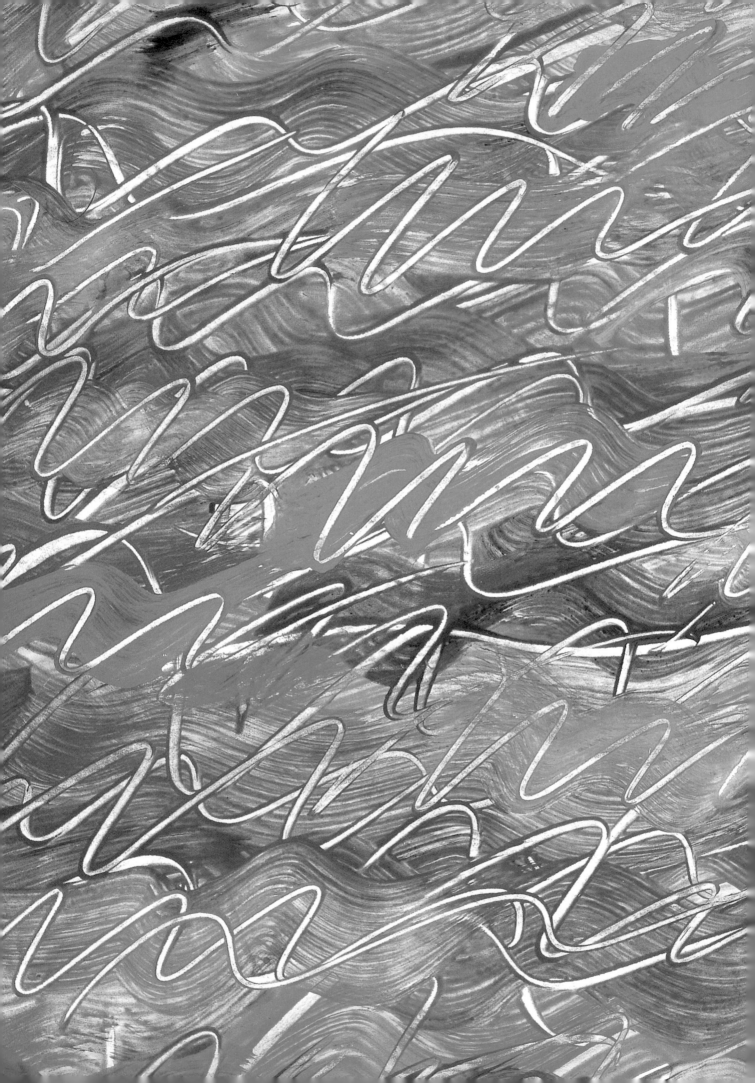

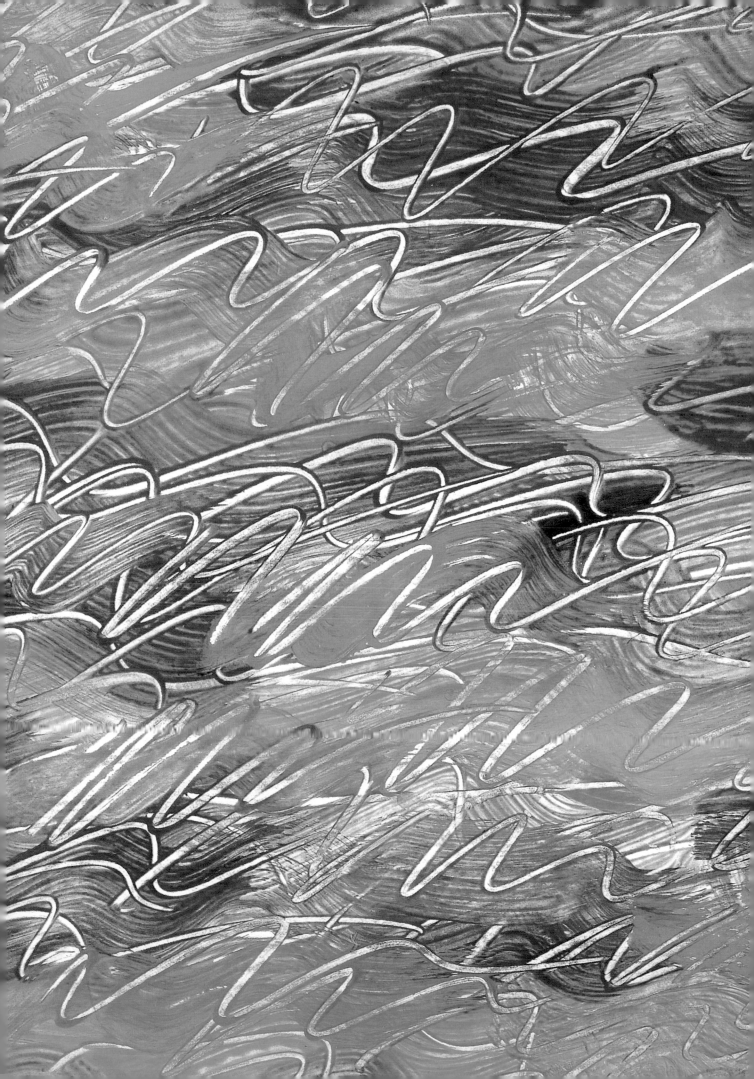

For my son Rolf

Hermit Crabs live
on the ocean floor.
Their skin is hard,
except for the abdomen,
which is soft.

To protect this "soft spot"
the hermit crab
borrows a shell and
makes this its "house."

Then only its face,
feet and claws stick out
from the shell.
That way, it can see,
walk and catch its food.

When a hermit crab
is threatened, it withdraws
into its shell until the
danger has passed.

A House for Hermit Crab

"Time to move," said Hermit Crab one day in January.
"I've grown too big for this little shell."

He had felt safe and snug in his shell. But now it was too snug.
Hermit Crab stepped out of the shell and onto the floor of the ocean.
But it was frightening out in the open sea without a shell to hide in.

"What if a big fish comes along and attacks me?" he thought.
"I must find a new house soon."

Early in February, Hermit Crab found just the house he was looking for. It was a big shell, and strong. He moved right in, wiggling and waggling about inside it to see how it felt. It felt just right.

"But it looks so—well, so *plain*," thought Hermit Crab.

In March, Hermit Crab met some sea anemones.
They swayed gently back and forth in the water.

"How beautiful you are!" said Hermit Crab.
"Would one of you be willing to come and live on my house?
It is so plain, it needs you."

"I'll come," whispered a small sea anemone.

Gently, Hermit Crab picked it up with his claw
and put it on his shell.

In April, Hermit Crab passed a flock of starfish moving slowly along the sea floor.

"How handsome you are!" said Hermit Crab.
"Would one of you be willing to decorate my house?"

"I would," signalled a little sea star.

Carefully, Hermit Crab picked it up with his claw and put it on his house.

In May, Hermit Crab discovered some coral.
They were hard, and didn't move.

"How pretty you are!" said Hermit Crab.
"Would one of you be willing to help
make my house more beautiful?"

"I would," creaked a crusty coral.

Gingerly, Hermit Crab picked it up with his claw and placed it on his shell.

In June, Hermit Crab came to a group of snails crawling over a rock on the ocean floor. They grazed as they went, picking up algae and bits of debris, and leaving a neat path behind them.

"How tidy and hard-working you are!" said Hermit Crab. "Would one of you be willing to come and help clean my house?"

"I would," offered one of the snails.

Happily, Hermit Crab picked it up with his claw and placed it on his shell.

In July, Hermit Crab came upon several sea urchins.
They had sharp, prickly needles.

"How fierce you look!" said Hermit Crab.
"Would one of you be willing to protect my house?"

"I would," answered a spiky sea urchin.

Gratefully, Hermit Crab picked it up with his claw
and placed it near his shell.

In August, Hermit Crab and his friends wandered into
a forest of seaweed. "It's so dark here," thought Hermit Crab.
"How dim it is," murmured the sea anemone.
"How gloomy it is," whispered the starfish.
"How murky it is," complained the coral.
"I can't see!" said the snail.
"It's like nighttime!" cried the sea urchin.

In September, Hermit Crab spotted a school of lanternfish darting through the dark water.

"How bright you are!" said Hermit Crab.
"Would one of you be willing to light up our house?"

"I would," replied one lanternfish. And it swam over near the shell.

In October, Hermit Crab approached a pile of smooth pebbles.

"How sturdy you are!" said Hermit Crab.
"Would you mind if I rearranged you?"

"Not at all," answered the pebbles.

Hermit Crab picked them up one by one with his claw
and built a wall around his shell.

"Now my house is perfect!" cheered Hermit Crab.

But in November, Hermit Crab felt that his shell seemed a bit too small. Little by little, over the year, Hermit Crab had grown. Soon he would have to find another, bigger home.
But he had come to love his friends, the sea anemone, the starfish, the coral, the sea urchin, the snail, the lanternfish, and even the smooth pebbles.

"They have been so good to me," thought Hermit Crab.
"They are like a family. How can I ever leave them?"

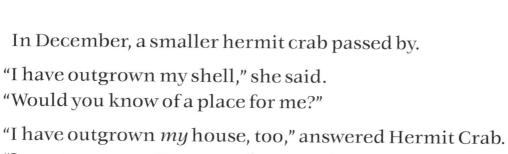

In December, a smaller hermit crab passed by.

"I have outgrown my shell," she said.
"Would you know of a place for me?"

"I have outgrown *my* house, too," answered Hermit Crab.
"I must move on. You are welcome to live here–
  but you must promise to be good to my friends."

"I promise," said the little crab.

The following January,
Hermit Crab stepped out and the little crab moved in.

"Couldn't stay in that little shell forever,"
said Hermit Crab as he waved goodbye.

The ocean floor looked wider
than he had remembered,
but Hermit Crab wasn't afraid.
Soon he spied the perfect house–
a big, empty shell. It looked, well,
a little plain, but...

"Sponges!" he thought.
"Barnacles! Clown fish! Sand dollars! Electric eels!
Oh, there are so many possibilities!
I can't wait to get started!"

Sea Anemones may look like flowers, but they are soft animals (polyps) without bony skeletons. They come in many shapes and colors. With their many arms (tentacles) they catch their prey. Some specialize in attaching themselves to the shell of the hermit crab. Then they protect and camouflage the hermit crab, and, in turn, may share the hermit crab's meals. This arrangement is called symbiosis, meaning that both animals benefit from each other.

Starfish. There are many kinds of starfish. Most have five arms growing from a central disk. The mouth of a starfish is on the underside of this disk, and it has a single, simple eye on the end of each arm. With its powerful arms it can open an oyster, or hold onto a rock during a storm when the waves lash about.

Corals are somewhat similar to tiny sea anemones that build hard skeletons around themselves. Then hundreds and hundreds of them stick together, forming whole colonies. Some look like branches; others are round or disk-like. Millions upon millions fuse themselves together to build miles-long coral reefs. Some, however, live by themselves.

Snails. There are approximately 80,000 species of snails and slugs. Some live on land, others live in the sea or in lakes. Some carry a shell–their "houses"–on their backs; others have none. The shells come in many colors and shapes.

Sea Urchins. Some are fat and round, others are thin and spindly. Many have long spines (sometimes poisonous) with which they move around and dig into the mud or rocks or other places. Their mouths, with five pointed teeth, are on the underside.

Lanternfish, like fireflies, have luminous, or light-producing, spots on their bodies that light up their dark surroundings. Some lanternfish have a lantern-like organ that dangles in front of their mouths, attracting other fish which become their prey.

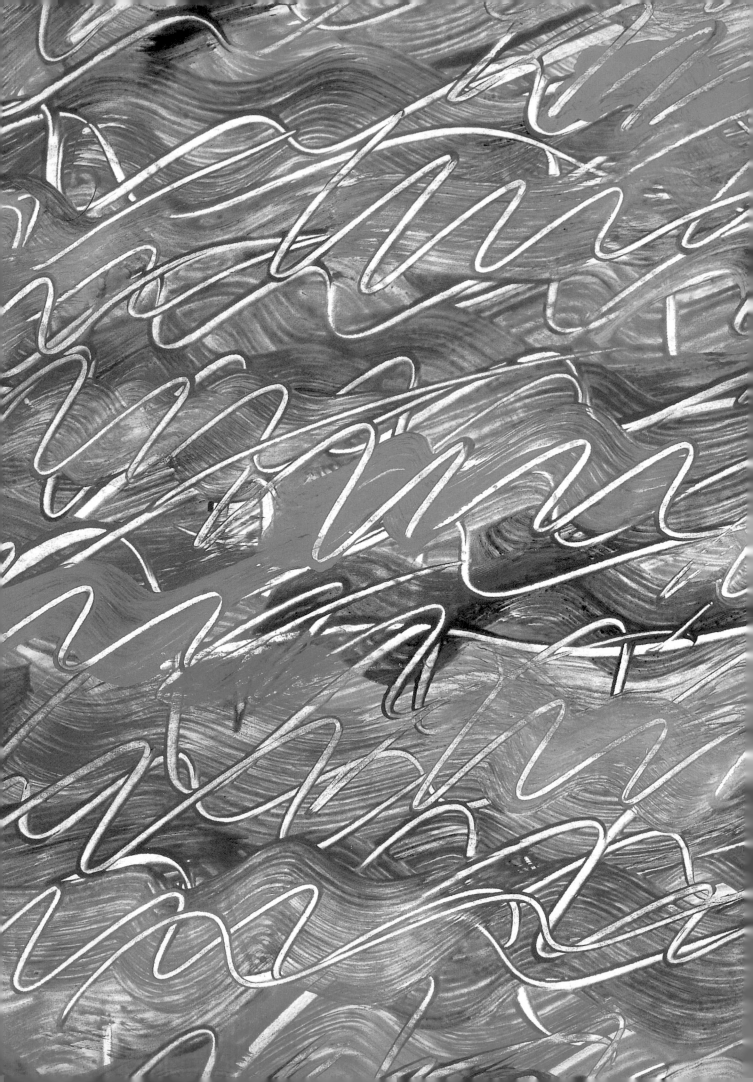

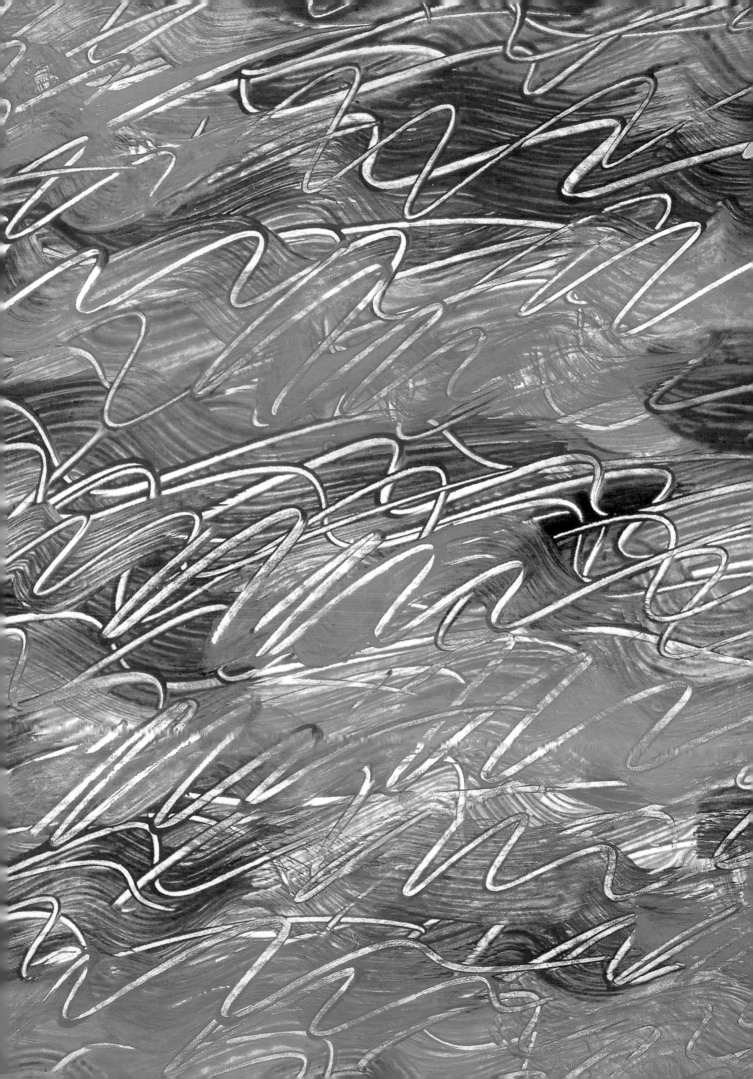

The Greedy Python

Richard Buckley

Eric Carle

The Greedy Python

by Richard Buckley
illustrated by Eric Carle

**Half hidden in the jungle green
The biggest snake there's ever been
Wound back and forth and in between.**

The giant snake was very strong
And very, very, very long.
He had a monstrous appetite,
His stomach stretched from left to right.

He quickly gobbled in one bite
Whatever creature came in sight:
A mouse that scampered to and fro,
A frog that jumped up from below,
A bat that hung from his left toe,
A fish that swam a bit too slow,
A bird that flew a bit too low,

A porcupine still half asleep,
A monkey who was in mid-leap,

A leopard sitting in a tree,
A buffalo who came to see.

An elephant, complete with trunk,
Was swallowed in a single chunk.
"I'm far too big to eat!" he cried.
"Oh, no you're not!" the snake replied.

At last the python's meal was done
And he lay resting in the sun.
The animals inside his skin
Were making quite a dreadful din;

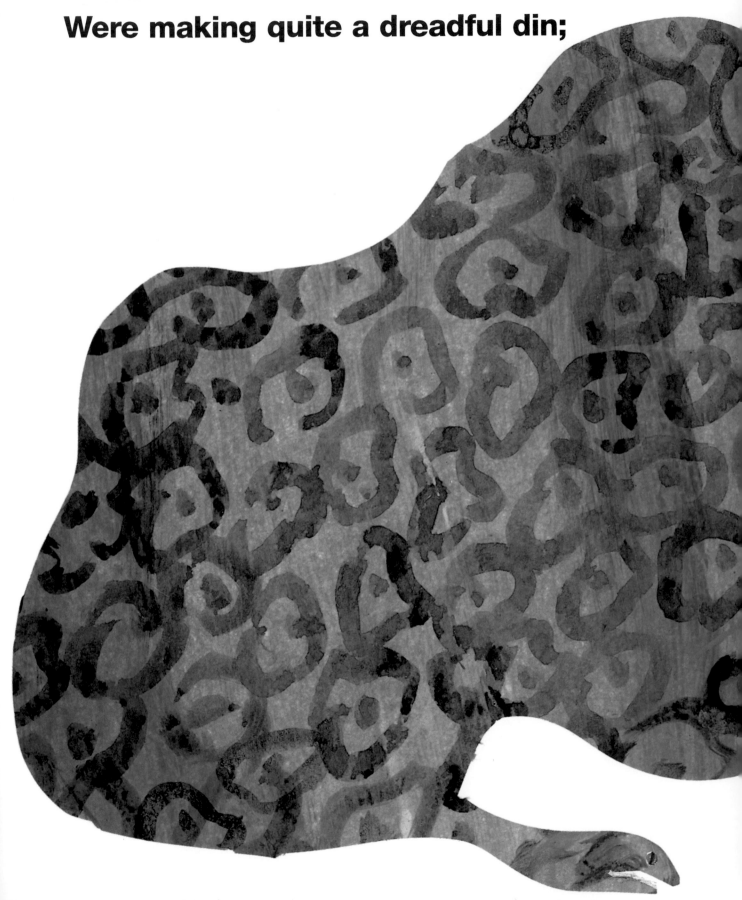

And when they all began to kick,
The snake began to feel quite sick.

He coughed the whole lot up again—
Each one of them—and there were ten.

He soon felt better, and what's more
Was hungrier than just before.
He hadn't learned a single thing:
His greed was quite astonishing.
He saw his own tail, long and curved,
And thought that lunch was being served.

He closed his jaws on his own rear
Then swallowed hard . . . and disappeared!

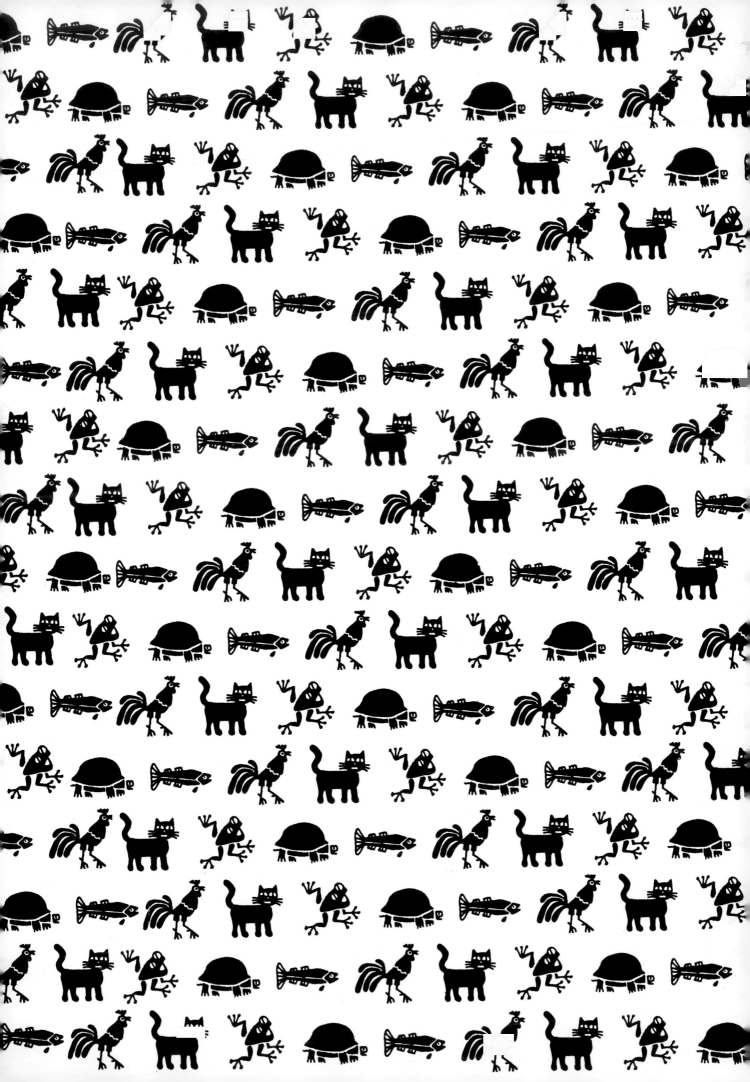

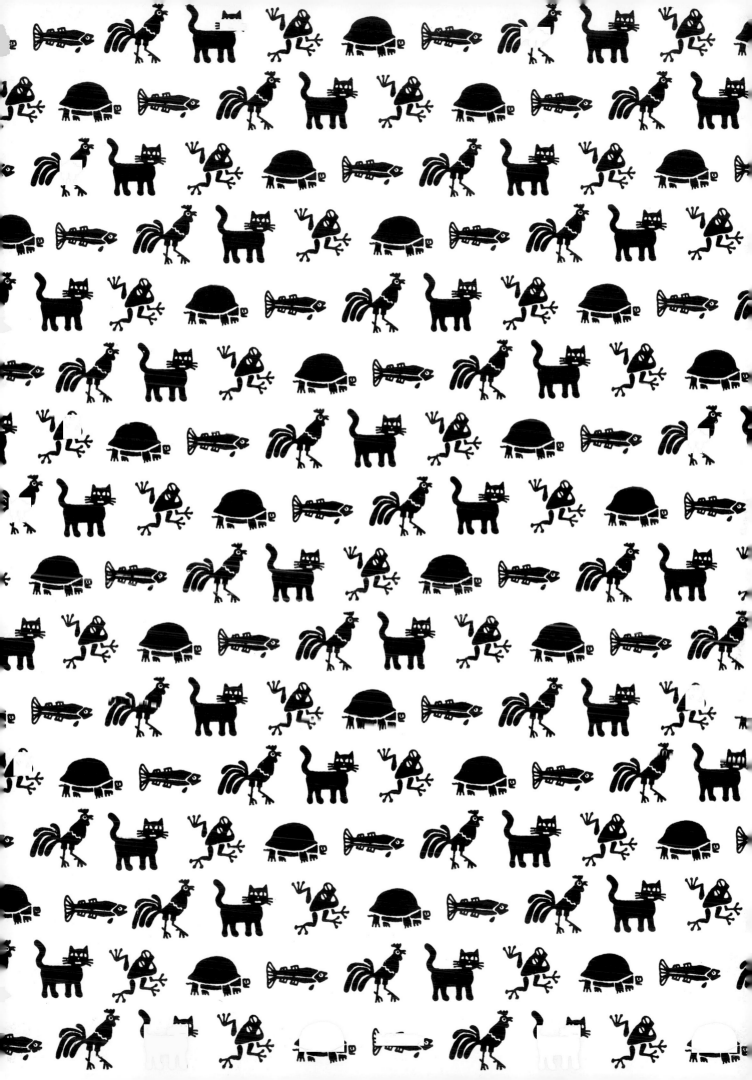

Rooster's Off
to See the World

ERIC CARLE

One fine morning, a rooster decided that he wanted to travel.
So, right then and there, he set out to see the world.
He hadn't walked very far when he began to feel lonely.

Just then, he met two cats. The rooster said
to them, "Come along with me to see the world."
The cats liked the idea of a trip very much.
"We would love to," they purred and set off down
the road with the rooster.

As they wandered on, the rooster and the cats met three frogs. "How would you like to come with us to see the world?" asked the rooster, eager for more company.
"Why not?" answered the frogs.
"We are not busy now." So the frogs jumped along behind the rooster and the cats.

After a while, the rooster, the cats, and the frogs saw four turtles crawling slowly down the road.

"Hey," said the rooster, "how would you like to see the world?"

"It might be fun," snapped one of the turtles and they joined the others.

As the rooster, the cats, the frogs, and the turtles walked
along, they came to five fish swimming in the brook.
"Where are you going?" asked the fish.
"We're off to see the world," answered the rooster.
"May we come along?" pleaded the fish.
"Delighted to have you," the rooster replied.
And so the fish came along to see the world.

The sun went down. It began to get dark. The moon came
up over the horizon. "Where's our dinner?" asked the cats.
"Where are we supposed to sleep?" asked the frogs.
"We're cold," complained the turtles.

Just then, some fireflies flew overhead. "We're afraid," cried the fish. Now, the rooster really had not made any plans for the trip around the world. He had not remembered to think about food and shelter, so he didn't know how to answer his friends.

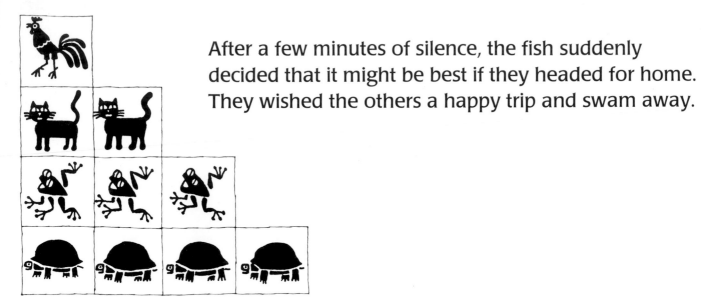

After a few minutes of silence, the fish suddenly decided that it might be best if they headed for home. They wished the others a happy trip and swam away.

Then, the turtles began to think about their warm house. They turned and crawled back down the road without so much as a good-bye.

The frogs weren't too happy with the trip anymore, either. First one and then the other and finally the last one jumped away. They were polite enough, though, to wish the rooster a good evening as they disappeared into the night.

The cats then remembered an unfinished meal they had left behind. They kindly wished the rooster a happy journey and they, too, headed for home.

Now the rooster was all alone – and he hadn't seen anything of the world. He thought for a minute and then said to the moon, "To tell you the truth, I am not only hungry and cold, but I'm homesick as well."
The moon did not answer. It, too, disappeared.

The rooster knew what he had to do.
He turned around and went back home again.
He enjoyed a good meal of grain and then sat
on his very own perch.

After a while he went to sleep and had a wonderful
happy dream – all about a trip around the world!

As a child, Eric Carle claims to have been much more of a philosopher than a mathematician. He recalls his difficulties this way:

"If you told me that there were two apples in a bowl and one was taken away and then asked me how many apples were left I wasn't sure. After all, you can't really take away an apple. You can eat it or make cider out of it or hide it under a basket, but the apple is still an apple and it isn't really gone...

"On the other hand, if you added one apple to a bowl with an apple already in it, there was always the bowl to worry about. Wasn't that a "something" to count in the total?"

Eric Carle wrote Rooster's Off to See the World *not only for the child who has these difficulties with numbers as specific symbols, but also for all children who are getting acquainted with numbers.*

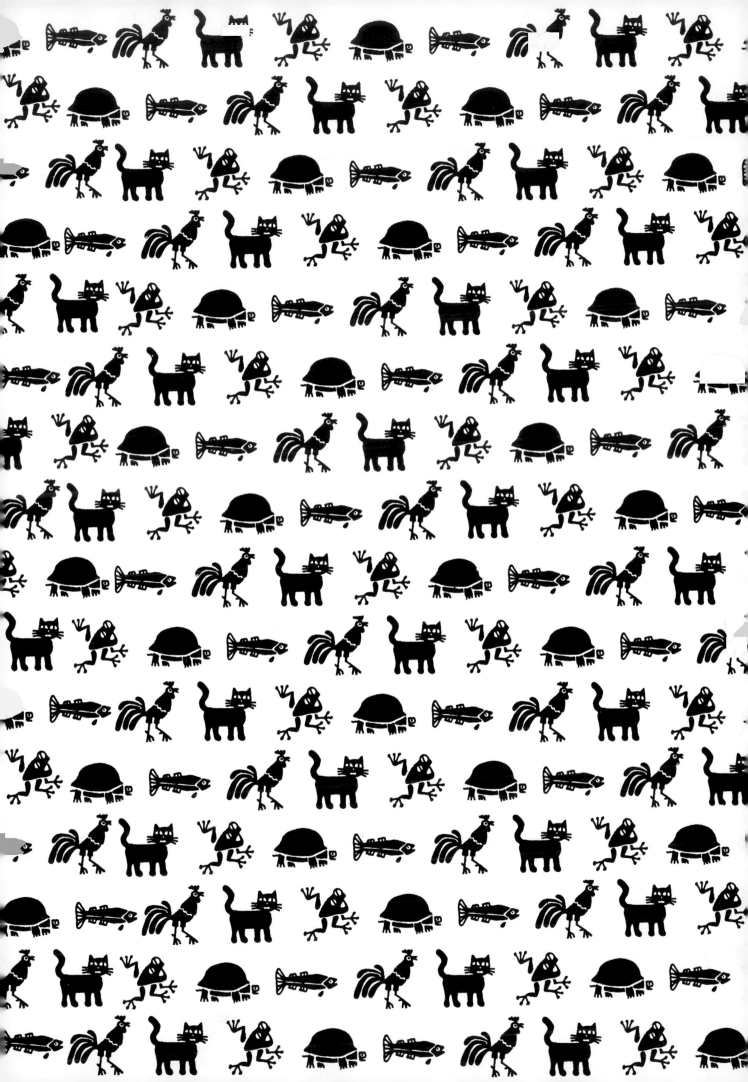

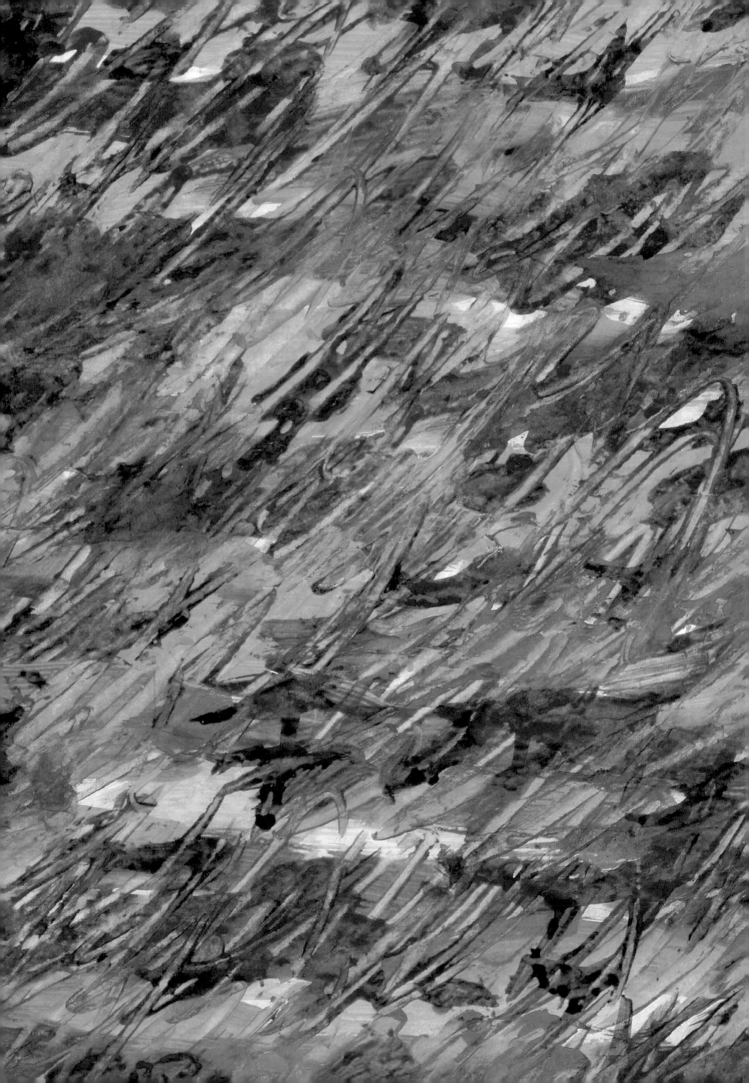